INFECTION POINTS

PRAISE FOR INFECTION POINTS

"Hangovers, poverty-stricken students, dangerous fieldwork, conservation biology, departmental politics, inter-lab rivalry—and vampires—all packed into less than a hundred pages. This is more than just a cool new take on the hoary old vampire trope: it's a pretty good portrait of grad school. Except the vampires are the study animals, not the administration."

—Peter Watts, award-winning author of *Blindsight*

"Pavlova pulls a remarkable trick: making vampires feel fascinating and vulnerable. Unnerving and eerie, *Infection Points* turns ecology into something dark, delivers a tense tale of secrets and disease, and proves why you shouldn't give academics a firearm."

—Haralambi Markov, author of *The Language of Knives*

"*Infection Points* is layered and complex, much like the relationship between humans and vampires that it posits."

—Alex Shvartsman, author of *The Best of All Possible Planets*

"Original and fiercely lean, *Infection Points* reimagines not only vampires, but the dangers of human agendas that depersonalize, control, and ultimately ravage marginalized communities."

—Dennis Mahoney, author of *Our Winter Monster and Dear Demons*

"*Infection Points* handles eco-horror, science, and vampires with unflinching practicality and compassion. I was truly riveted from start to finish."

—Mercedes M. Yardley, three-time Bram Stoker Award-winning author of *Darling*

"*Infection Points* provides a unique and fascinating perspective on vampirism, exploring the socio-economic impact of these urban predators in Bulgaria by blending horror with academia and science with myth. The story introduces many intriguing concepts, both novel and borrowed from Balkan lore, to create a world not too far removed from our own that demands greater exploration. A curious reader will no doubt find this novella only whets the appetite, fueling the hunger for more stories where vampires are not only the subject of ethically dubious academic study but also the unwitting victims of complex human ecopolitics."

—Xan van Rooyen, award-winning author of *Born of Malice* and *Waypoint Seven*

"In *Infection Points,* Pavlova delivers a poignant dose of dark satire about those infected and affected by a deadly contagion. Funny, heartfelt, and terrifying—an entertaining antidote for readers looking for fast-paced eco-horror."

—J. R. Blanes, author of *Portraits of Decay*

INFECTION POINTS

A WINTER CENSUS OF URBAN PREDATORS

ELENA
PAVLOVA

TRANSLATED FROM THE BULGARIAN
BY ROBERTA BASARBOLIEVA,
ELENA PAVLOVA,
AND KALIN M. NENOV

RUADÁN
BOOKS

BOSTON, MA

Infection Points: A Winter Census of Urban Predators

ISBN 978-1-968143-31-2 (trade paperback)
ISBN 978-1-968143-32-9 (ebook)
ISBN 978-1-968143-33-6 (audiobook)
Library of Congress Control Number: 2026937300

Edited by Maria Haskins
Cover Illustration by Kip Ayers
Design/Formatting by Leah Donell

First Edition

RUADÁN
BOOKS

RuadanBooks.com

To all my friends from the
writers' workshop in Melnik 2015

Despite what the weathermen said, February wasn't that cold. The weather was perfect for grabbing my Nikon Z5II and wandering the neighborhood in the morning twilight. After all, I only saw the sunrise during a quarter of the year.

I paused next to the daycare and watched the smoke rising from its central heating chimney. It was past six, and the canteen ladies had begun their mysterious dance. The yogurt delivery truck pulled into the yard—the never-changing rhythms of ordinary life.

Out of habit, I looked up at my windows—they were the only lit ones in Block 10 at this hour—and I saw someone standing on *that* balcony in the next section. Section C jutted forward, so you could peek at your neighbors from the narrow side of their balconies. *Their* apartment had a glass-enclosed balcony, but two years ago, a hole had appeared in the glass above the cement cornice, and the girl peered out sometimes. It was her habit to watch the muscle-bound truck driver unload the yogurt at the daycare, but now she was looking straight at my balcony and the silver chain with crosses adorning the door. The winter wind tugged at the wide sleeves of her blue nightdress.

She shouldn't have been awake at all: *they* should be hibernating at this time. I didn't mean just today. Like bats, vampires slept their winter sleep between November and March.

I went numb, to say the least. Slowly raising the camera, I took a few shots. I zoomed in to inspect her better, and—yes—the camera screen displayed her death sentence: her whole cheek was crisscrossed with red scratch marks over a yellowish patch. I took a couple more shots, but the stabilizer couldn't handle the magnification and my shaking hands.

The girl retreated into *her* apartment without turning towards the truck at the daycare. She didn't notice me either.

It suddenly felt like −10°C and, by the time I got into Section B, my eyes were burning. From the cold.

I sent the pics off to London for confirmation, brewed myself some coffee, and waited. Until now, we hadn't had a case of *Candida vampiris* here in Mihaylovgrad, in Bulgaria, or even in the Balkans. Except for that forum rumor.

Around 7:20, Chefo phoned from Ruse to assure me he was ready to head my way as soon as I called. I could hear him rustling; he put down his cup and tapped the keyboard a few times.

"Is that the spyhole?" he asked, clicking his mouse. "The floor above is easier to vault to. Why is she watching yours?"

I heard him raise his cup and clink its rim against the saucer. Chefo was like that: even at home, he took his coffee in a china set. He used a coaster too.

"Why was she looking for you?" He blew at his cup and took a sip.

According to my diploma, I'd graduated in ecology from Sofia University, but even before the end of my first year, I got pulled into Conservation of Urban Predators. At university, I'd never imagined a future of hanging around a lousy apartment in the sole company of nu metal and thin coffee, feet propped on the oil radiator, waiting for someone at the other end of the world to confirm that the fungus on my vampire's cheek was indeed *vampiris*. Yet here I was: one of probably twenty living inhabitants in Block 10 and definitely the only one who slept with a tranquilizer rifle loaded with silver nitrate by his bed.

"I know the girl," I confessed. "And she knows who I am and what I do."

"You're nuts!" Chefo said. "You'll make me choke."

"Why? They're still here, aren't they?"

He swallowed, put down his cup—a sharp tinkle—and said, "I greet some of the guys in the nest next door, too. We're their observers, after all. I also know a couple of their Bites."

The email notifier on my screen was blinking. It was my turn to choke on the coffee: London refused a positive identification and wanted a sample before taking a decision on elimination. I swore and burst into hysterical laughter.

There was a crash on the other end of the line. In the suspicious silence, I asked, "Are you OK? What happened?"

"I fell off my chair, frak you!" snapped Chefo. "What happened to *you*? You startled me."

Frak me? I sniggered. On the other end, there was scraping and a clink.

"I'm back," said Chefo. "Spit it out, I'm all ears."

"Do you have any doubts?" I asked. "Judging by the pics? Because apparently our superiors do and they want me to catch them some shrooms."

Chefo paused, puffed over his coffee, took a sip. Finally, he asked, "Are you going to the lair on your own? You know the protocol."

"It'll be late afternoon by the time we all gather. Either way, we'll see each other for the elimination." I coughed. My throat caught. "Anyway, what the hell, I'm just gonna scrape myself a sample, not flirt with the vamps!"

Chefo grunted in agreement but didn't laugh.

Throughout the history of humanity, house spirits like bogeys, brownies, and kobolds had always cohabited with us in our common spaces, playing a substantial role in both our lives and folklore. They had always been hunted, their numbers quickly diminishing during the Industrial Era.

Vampires were a special case. They were the biggest species. Apex urban predators with a nocturnal way of life and very sophisticated nesting systems. Now, in the 21st century, their dependency on humans as hosts and food had pushed them to the brink of extinction. That's why we were here, crackpots like Chefo and me, and a load of other mytho-ecologists. House spirits were now considered extinct, but vampires still had a chance.

Or at least they used to have one until Dave Matthews came across the first cases of *Candida vampiris* in Panama in 1995. Tony—my boss—hit the roof each time somebody came up with new, cheerier fabrications on that topic, each more harmful than the previous. Most often, "somebody" meant our colleagues from the World Urban Predators Fund; for a couple of years, they'd even been applying an experimental "treatment" on vamps in Belgium. Pathetic stuff, not worth fretting over. Who were they trying to deceive anyway?

I finished my coffee, gathered my stuff in a frayed sports bag, changed the compressed air cartridge in the rifle, and hung the camera around my neck. The keyring hung on a nail in the corridor all year round.

Vampire lairs made a pitiful sight, even when you were used to them. On the noticeboard by the Section B foyer, several soaked obituaries fluttered in the wind, all young faces. There were typically fewer parked cars in front of our building than anywhere in town, but as I walked towards the door of the next section, I realized that the snow had not been shoveled off most of the vehicles. The dumpsters gaped empty, the same pink plastic bag waving from a lid for the third week running. Did I say twenty living inhabitants? I'd overestimated by a long shot.

I unlocked the metal door and waded through a sea of flyers, which should've been shoveled out long ago. Usually the Bites did that. Officially, Bites were called "recurrent blood donors" and at least five or six tended to gravitate around each nest, often more. Bites were the day-eyes of the nest. Low-dose, repeated exposure had been proven to keep them from turning into vampires immediately. Theirs was a life of misery and enslavement, and I'd kept track of them for a few years now.

The entrance stank of piss, mold, and carrion. I took the biohazard suit out of my bag and struggled into it. The chemical taste of the filtered air came as a massive relief. I started up the stairs slowly, without bothering to check if the elevator still worked.

Though the flyers had already set off some alarm bells, I got *really* worried by the little pile of bones on the landing between the second and third floors. I raised my camera and got down to it. Exposed to direct sunlight, vampires didn't actually disintegrate instantly and definitely didn't turn to ash. Judging by the dirt-gray windows, this one had fought to scrabble outside even when the pain should have chased him back to the comfortable darkness of the lair.

Vampires didn't do such things.

I took out a plastic bag from the sample case and diligently dropped in a couple of tiny bones with some material on them. Judging by the checked shirt and the jeans, the vampire was indeed one of the males.

Who lay here: Jordan or Barefoot?

The bag with the samples went into the bio-isolation pocket, and I was just tugging the zipper closed when I thought I heard something rustling on the floor above. I grabbed the rifle and aimed so fast that the connecting motion didn't register. I told myself off for my fried nerves and climbed the first two steps very carefully, never diverting my sights from the upper landing.

It was physically impossible for vampires to be wide awake in broad daylight. You learned that in the first lectures on urban predators. Vampires just didn't do such things.

Dessita jumped me at the next step. She wasn't screaming only because there was nothing left to scream with: her decayed throat released a hiss like a boiling kettle. She'd been curled up in the darkest corner of the landing, next to the elevator door, and even so the light had eaten her flesh down to the bones.

I shot her point-blank, and the silver basically set her on fire, that's how gone she was. Her body lit up in dry white flames and burned to ashes with a quiet *Pssshtt*, while I shook and relearned how to breathe. Fuck—vampires did not do such things!

The phone vibrated madly in my pocket.

Now what?

The camera! The damn helmet had a built-in camera. Had I turned it on? Who the hell was watching me?

My heart was downright skipping from the vibration. The Vampoodles' "Tender is the Blood" got louder and louder, echoing along the staircase.

"Fuck!" I tugged at the zipper of my suit.

I saw him from the corner of my eye—or rather, I felt him by the stirring of the shadows. Clumsily, I swiped the rifle upwards. The trigger clicked on empty. I hadn't reloaded, and anyway I had no chance of hitting the monster collapsing on me from the ceiling. This whole time, he'd been hanging off the staircase light fixture. The rifle's muzzle smashed into his face and twisted his head sideways—and then his skeletal hands got hold of me, his knees slamming into my stomach. I lost my balance and reeled backwards down the stairs, flailing the weapon blindly.

My phone kept wailing in my pocket.

The top of my head barely missed the windowsill, but the rifle smashed into the window with a loud crash. As daylight splashed through the shattered glass, the vampire screamed and twisted. Nevertheless, his teeth found the edge of my helmet. The lens of my camera dug into his ribs, preventing him from ripping into me straightaway. I couldn't breathe from the pain but still managed to smash the rifle into him. My other hand patted at the suit pockets, found the jet injectors, and stuck one into him, just as my movement caught his attention and he turned his head to close his jaws around my wrist. I felt him pierce the suit sleeve as he lit up in a bright white flame.

"Fuck!" I managed finally, coughed, and slid the rest of the way down.

The phone had shut up. I had no idea when.

There were no further surprises between the third and the fourth floors.

Only discoveries.

This time I reloaded the rifle and carefully inspected the upper floor before retreating to the landing with the broken window and the remains of the three vampires. Only then did I change my gloves, remove the upper half of my suit, and disinfect the bite. The wound was bleeding profusely and didn't start decomposing in the sun, which was a good sign, but while applying the silver spray, I wanted to cut my hand off. I screamed and jumped around while the foam seethed and bubbled. I squeezed half a tube of antibiotic cream on top and wrapped everything in a thick layer of bandages. The wound kept hurting like nobody's business even after I stuffed my arm back in the suit's sleeve, but at least the bleeding was more or less under control.

I took my phone out of my jeans pocket and did what I should have done in the first place: connected it by Bluetooth to the headphones in the damn helmet. The camera wasn't transmitting—at least there would be no record of my antics—and the missed call was from Tony. I dug through the bag, took out wet wipes, cleaned up the snot and tears, and didn't return his call. Let him fume as he pleased; I had no strength for any portion of normality right now.

I pulled the zipper, shouldered the bag, and… continued upwards. Yeah, yeah, I know what the rules say, but if I went back to deal with the wound and call for backup, this sample business would drag on for at least two more days. There'd be too much risk of a sick specimen escaping and causing the loss of Northwest Bulgaria's entire vampire population, or maybe worse. Plus, how would I muster the courage to come back?

All the apartments on the third floor were locked. On the next landing, I found the remains of a victim, perhaps the reason for the carrion smell downstairs. Was this the Bite in charge of the flyers? I fought off the desire to turn on the helmet camera, grabbed my Nikon, and took a couple of shots. The old man was shriveled and mummified, so it was hard to tell how many bites he had, but I could see several sets of teeth marks on him.

On the floor of the actual lair, there was another fried vampire, and the door of the middle apartment was broken and left ajar.

Vampires do not do such things! The words scraped desperately through my head in time with the pulsing pain of my wound. All winter I, the grand savior of urban fauna, had blissfully listened to music with my feet on the radiator, while the shit had been rising towards the fan.

I put down my bag, left it by the elevator, and climbed to the eighth floor just in case, but I didn't find any further surprises. Vampires had nothing in common with cats: blind panic didn't lead them to higher ground.

I returned to the fourth floor, turned on the front spotlight of the helmet, and pushed the door of the middle apartment with the rifle. The hallway was dim and devoid of ambush. Under the bathroom sink, touchingly hugging a pillow, slept a skeletal black-haired man. He hadn't been on my census last year, but I realized that I knew him: I'd seen him around the neighborhood and had made him out to be the right type for a Bite. Stiff with nerves, I poked him with the rifle, but—as good little vampires do—he did not react: only his hand slipped out from under the pillow as if freshly released from rigor mortis.

The back of the hand was dotted with white specks and crisscrossed by angry red lines where he'd scratched at them with his jagged nails.

I carefully took out the sample set, squatted down, dug the rifle's muzzle under the kid's chin, and scraped a bit of *vampiris* from his hand. He was so new that I even got a drop of blood. I took a second sample from a spot above his wrist. Poor bastard: they caught the fungus even easier when fresh.

I returned everything to my pockets and was just backing off when the vampire shifted. I don't know if the fungus itched too much, or if it made his hibernation lighter than usual and he'd smelled me, but his face wrinkled and his hand twitched.

The rifle might've held only compressed air, but in the small bathroom the shot thundered like a cannon blast. I ran out of the apartment without watching the kid burn up.

It was strange, the way people integrated with vampires. Perhaps this was the hardest part to grasp at university. If a lair showed up somewhere, a community soon gathered around it. A daycare would sprout up, a school, a hospital. In this sense, vampires were a unique species. Our profs told us this stemmed from the improved psychological climate around the lairs, but when I moved here to Mikhaylovgrad, I thought the whole situation unnatural. It was clear that if I started trumpeting, "Run, there're vampires here!" someone would question my own psychological climate, but… innocent children playing right next to the predators' jaws? This was something I struggled with, even if the children were safe during the day, and even if the area near the lair was deserted at night (except for the Bites living close by).

It was a fact, though, that no vampires had ever been chased by mobs with torches. Quite the opposite, like the historical case in Manchester where a consecrated company sent by the bishop to hunt the local vampires had been kicked out of the city. Moreover, the research indicated that if we allowed *Candida vampiris* to spread over the Balkans, the emigration rates would probably go up even more than they already had as people left the infection points in search of a better habitat. One with its urban predators intact.

Was there any truth in the rumors on that French forum? Tony had written them off with an angry grimace: "Just another lie!" But wherever there was smoke, there had to be fire, and I'd already seen four posts claiming that an entire Bulgarian lair had been eliminated last winter. Ridiculous, of course; Maya in Pazardzhik wouldn't hide such a thing from us. Right?

I was still struggling with that *right,* when, after a long shower and a new bandage, it turned out it was only 9:30. I rinsed a glass and splashed in a generous measure of whiskey. The first sip burned like silver, but at least it warmed me up and stopped my teeth from chattering. I still needed to get dressed, pack the damn samples, and send them out by courier. After the second sip, I manned up enough to raise my feet onto the radiator, lean back in my chair, and call Tony.

Tony, aka Anton Deliyski, Professor of Comparative Biology and an expert in urban predators, was the boss of the Bulgarian branch of Urban Predators without Borders, which had been paying my wages for quite a few years. All my official mail went out with a BCC to him, so I wasn't surprised when he skipped the intros and rumbled, "You haven't done something stupid, have you?" And, because he knew his people well, Tony interpreted my hesitation correctly and interrupted my mumbling. "What did you do, you dunderhead? How many times have I told you to keep the camera on, huh? Are you alright?"

"Yep," I managed to reply.

"Yep as in 'I got away with just a bit of a fright,' or yep as in 'Tonight I'm gonna turn?'"

"I got a bit nibbled," I confessed. I downed the rest of my drink and hoarsely explained, "Tony, you've no idea how bad things are. They're *bad*. I feel like smashing my head open on that wall I share with their apartment! I never noticed anything. I won't forgive myself, I will not."

I shivered. I'd already had nightmares, thanks very much! I didn't want to be part of the elimination team. I didn't want any elimination team at all on the fourth floor. I put down the glass and gently took my feet off the radiator.

"How bad is it, on a scale of one to ten?" asked Tony. He tried to speak calmly. I would've bought it if his voice hadn't quivered.

I giggled. "Bad? We're drowning in a fucking cesspool! It's the big shit, Tony. It looks like that video from Denver, and I didn't even enter the main lair. Hold on, I gotta pour myself another."

"Holding," said Tony, and I giggled again. My hands shook, almost dropping the bottle, because the silver ointment had finally eaten its way to living flesh, and the pain was unimaginable. I managed to pour the drink and told myself I would call a courier to pick up the samples for my peace of mind. With a bite like that, and the drinks in my belly, I wouldn't be able to drive to the shipping company anyway.

Denver, 2007. The documentary was filmed by Dave Matthews and commissioned by the US Department of Fish and Wildlife Conservation (the Urban Fauna section). It bore the *Top Secret* sigil and covered a three-year observation period of a nest with, originally, 47 vampires, located in a small three-story building in a cozy neighborhood. At that time, I'd thought my nightmares would never stop: in the end, the National Guard was brought in to eliminate the last of the *vampiris* victims, who, as it turned out, were still alive. They hunted them down as far as three blocks away from the nest, among the remains of half-eaten bodies. The frenzied feeding was the grizzliest side effect of the infection. Since then, Predators without Borders had maintained a strict protocol of elimination at the first sight of contagion.

I pressed my bandaged hand to my chest—the human instinct to seek a healing contact with a living body—actually, in Supernatural Biology, you learn early on that the analgesic quality of touch has been scientifically proven. I took a sip. A small one. "Last year everything was fine," I said imploringly. "Right?"

Meto and Maya had come for the late February census, we filmed the whole process meticulously, took photos, catalogued…

"It was fine," Tony said grumpily. "And that's not just your opinion and not just your nest."

"We've missed something," I mumbled, and a second small sip followed the first.

I was still seeing scenes from the 2007 documentary. Worse, I was seeing scenes from Phoenix and Baltimore, in addition to Denver: all cities that had also lost their vampire populations. Because of the fungus, over two hundred vampires had been eliminated in Paris and its suburbs, almost a third of the French population.

Remove the wolves from a forest and the deer will run rampant, eating all saplings and even the bark from the trees. Remove the urban predators from the cities and…

For the second time, I exchanged a look with the bottom of my glass. Tony and I still hadn't said anything substantial. I changed the subject. "Listen, I know we can gather as early as this afternoon, but it'll be dark, Tony, so don't come, do you hear? You better send our guys to check their own nests first."

"And you? You'd better go to a hotel in Vratsa."

"Why? What's changed since last night? I'm protected just fine." This time I didn't even make him stay on the line as I filled my glass.

Both of us knew what had changed: last night, I hadn't killed three vampires. But the situation was so bad I doubted the remaining ones would even notice my intrusion. And I was well protected, considering *they* hadn't come knocking on my door, despite being starved.

A courier and a bottle of whiskey later, it was still 10:40. The advantages of a small town: I called the taxi service to stock up on booze. A small tip gave drivers enough courage to get close to Block 10. I paid, hung the silver chains and crosses back up, and saw that my email notifier was blinking again. The message was marked *Urgent*, and the title contained the word *Mihaylovgrad*. I clicked it. Was London confirming the initial identification, making my morning adventure redundant?

Hello, my name is Magdalena Manolova, and I manage

the Bulgarian branch of the World Urban Predators Fund.

One of our teams will be in Mihaylovgrad within hours, and ***we have a cure****! Just give us an address. We can save the nest!*

Please do not let them be eliminated!

Please!

Allow us to save them!

—M. Manolova, World Urban Predators Fund, Bulgaria

I stared at the message, which the whiskey had emptied of meaning. In fact, the subject was *Je suis Mihaylovgrad*. I opened a new bottle and poured myself a generous amount. Then I clicked *Reply* and wrote my address and phone number.

Please…

In a drunken surge of genius, I turned off the automatic BCC before pressing send.

Then I switched back to YouTube and clicked on Vampoodles' "Re/Birth."

I emptied my glass and poured myself another drink. I was still able to find my mouth.

A ballad began. My eyes stung.

Please!

What woke me up was the vibration of my phone,

rather than the first bars of the song blaring out of my pocket. I blinked painfully in the dusk. According to the screen, it was only 5 PM or so, and I had three emails in my inbox. My head wasn't trying to split in two yet, but I'd almost reached the bottom of the second bottle, so it was just a matter of time. For the moment, however, my skull was full of cotton, and *the blaring song* burrowed a path through it, connecting "phone" with "pocket." I dug out the pulsating pest and stabbed the green receiver.

"Get lost."

"I'm Maggie Manolova, we exchanged a couple of emails..."

The notifier assured me the three new emails were all hers.

"Do you mind if we come up to your apartment? It's getting dark."

I groaned.

"We can come back tomorrow, of course," Maggie said. "I'm just really worried it will be too late."

She wasn't wrong. Even through the whiskey fog, I worried about the same thing.

I surveyed the usual mess and remembered the empty fridge. "I don't know how many of you there are," I mumbled, "but I have nothing but eggs."

"There're four of us. Shall we... get something for you too?"

"I'll put on some coffee," I decided after a couple seconds. "Wait, I'll toss you the keys."

I bruised my hip on the kitchen table, fumbled for quite a while with the window, and leaned over the sill.

Maggie was a brunette. She didn't wear a hat. Her team traveled in an unmarked minivan. A guy in a checkered ski jacket stood at the back door, saying, "...sausages. And juice."

My stomach cramped. As I turned on the coffee machine, I felt like the threadworms in my belly were starting a riot. I dug through the cupboard, found a forgotten croissant, and just as I bit down on it, I heard my key scraping in the front door lock.

The croissant turned out to be dry, almost crunchy, and it stuck in my throat as I tried to swallow it. This was how Maggie and the guy in the checkered jacket found me: with hamster cheeks, unable to even greet them. When she put out her hand, I was still holding the half-eaten croissant. What a dimple Maggie had on her chin! We looked at each other, until Checkered Jacket saved me. "You already know our Maggie. I'm Peter. I've read your reports and seen you around on the forums. Glad to finally meet you in person."

I gave a questioning mumble, my mouth still full.

"Peter Berkovski," Maggie said and went around me to close the gaping window.

I finally managed my mouthful and said, "Pleasure. The Paris scandal, right?"

It wasn't like we didn't occasionally read forums, too.

"The successful restoration of the Paris population," Peter corrected. He spoke as if lecturing. "Our nest this year has thirty-two vampires, and we're going to set up a second nest in the spring."

I took out cups and started brewing coffee. I remembered Tony's white-hot rage when the Fund wrestled their way to the French lair experiment.

"In Belgium we're treating the entire population," said Maggie. "For the third year running."

We didn't have a branch in Belgium. Tony constantly complained that Belgium was the breeding ground for *vampiris* in Europe because of our competitors' wimpy policies, and that the whole country had to be burned down if we wanted to save the species.

"I don't think I have sugar." I handed the first cup to the lady as the machine worked on the second one.

"I like it black." Maggie smiled and took the cup in both hands. She and Peter hadn't taken off their jackets. I knew the apartment was cold but I only used the living room.

"The big problem," said Peter, reaching for the second coffee, "is that the medicine isn't a vaccine. It doesn't create immunity."

"They get infected again," said Maggie. "This winter we had new cases in Paris."

I felt like throwing up. The kitchen table bruised me again before I reached the sink and leaned over it, but the croissant refused to come up.

Vampires maddened by the fungus. Causing indiscriminate casualties… struggling to enlarge their nest without understanding that the newly turned would also get infected and die in short order… while those guys at the World Fund benevolently did nothing. Treating the population… as if!

"But the failed robbery at *Le Crédit Lyonnais* showed it's worth treating them," Peter said. "It was also our first time documenting the benefits of vampires in natural conditions."

I was still leaning over the sink, bathed in a cold sweat, but I turned and raised my eyebrows.

"The bank office of LCL," Peter added. "Are you going to have that coffee?"

"What about *Le Crédit* Whatever?" I snorted. I poured myself some water. The first ice-cold sip nailed itself to my stomach.

Maggie sized me up, bit her lip, and asked, "Are you playing stupid or have you really not followed the case? Even Professor Deliyski commented on the video that it was 'impressive.'"

Hogwash. Next she'd tell me her and Tony regularly caught up over drinks and she'd have me totally fooled.

"Some of our vampires moved the evening before the planned strike at the LCL bank office," Peter explained calmly, taking a sip of coffee. "The nest tracked the robbers once they began rehearsing. We found four victims, only one terminal. And voila, the robbery never happened."

"There was a similar operation in Belgium a month later, most of the participants were arrested," Maggie said. "But the nests there are preserved. And in November we were lucky to have warm weather, even though some of the vampires were already hibernating."

I dumped the glass in the sink with unnecessary force. "Oh stop it! Get out! That does it, taking credit for such a piece of cr—"

I couldn't finish as acid rose in my throat, and this time I parted with the croissant. The whiskey dregs too. I went on dry-heaving over the sink.

When the world blurred before my eyes and I staggered, Peter grabbed me and helped me sit down. The kitchen was spinning and tilting.

I'd seen the failed robbery in Paris as an out-and-out tragedy. Apparently, I should have seen it as a barely-avoided catastrophe.

Maggie walked out. Peter handed me the third cup

of coffee, stood by the window, and let me drink it in small sips while I frowned at the taste. I heard a noise in the corridor and a couple of voices: their two pals had returned from the store.

"Do you communicate with your vampires?" Peter asked at some point.

"They aren't the safest of buddies to gab with."

"Yes or no?" He smiled, knowing what the answer would be. "More coffee?"

"Yes. Definitely yes."

My stomach was still mutinying, but I needed the coffee. I'd recently happened across a study that claimed that coffee after a drunken stupor solidified the intoxication rather than cleared the mind, but it had always had a good effect on me.

"Do you have contact with the leader?" said Peter.

"I think I found him this morning." I remembered the jeans-clothed remains and swallowed. The coffee made my throat dry as parchment.

For a while, Peter stared outside again, where the winter dusk gently stroked the pink plastic bag on the dumpster. "And the little one? Didi? It's her in the photos, isn't it?"

"Yeah. It's her." I frowned. "You did read my reports, huh?"

"Didn't I tell you they're impressive? You don't believe me or what?"

"How on earth did you even get them?" I put the cup on the table to avoid spilling it. Anger healed me better than coffee. "Is there a mole among us? Don't you have any…" I meant to say "shame," but of course, it was absurd to expect the enemy to play fair.

"Rubbish!" Peter grinned. "The exchange of data between your people at Without Borders and us at the World Fund is quite official. Don't tell me you don't have our reports and the rest."

"No, I don't!" I raised my voice. "And we have nothing to do with you, cut the lies! I know you're keen on treating my vampires. I've invited you to treat them, dammit…"

I had no more strength to be angry. I just felt low. Blinking hard, I took a sip and forced the coffee through my tight throat. "There's no point. No point at all. You better leave. If you can't cure them once and for all, why do I need you? They're gonna die anyway."

The kitchen door opened a crack, and a shaggy blond head peeked through. "Is it safe? I bring peace offerings." The newcomer smiled.

Peter raised his eyebrows at me. I didn't nod, but he said, "Come in! This is Gogo," he told me. "He's a junior student at the university."

"You're doing a fantastic job here!" The kid burst in with two huge bags, gave me a shy grin, and started taking out salads and bread.

Fuck, did the whole World Fund know about my humble self?

"Shall we get out of Gogo's way?" Peter said. "Come, let's go to the other room. So what were you saying about Didi?"

Another coffee and half a warm hot dog later, it still wasn't even 6:30, but the darkness outside the windows was thick as gelatin. From my spot, I could see that Maggie's people had hung extra protection on the balcony. The fourth member of their team was Sonia Volny, a volunteer from Dresden, who spoke English with a heavy accent and would fit in a word of Bulgarian here and there. She shuttled between the kitchen and the living room, bringing the food that had finally started coming from the stove and the party grill.

"It has to work if you think she can read," Peter told me and opened the printer menu on my computer. "Should I print it?"

I nodded.

I wasn't aware of any studies on the abilities vampires retained from their initial human host. The whole turning process had been sketchily studied, and only in the past few years had we seen several more solid studies. Until 2001, no one even understood how the mechanism of turning worked. Except for the rule that it took three nights to rise from the coffin. And that the repeated blood donations from the Bites delayed the turning process for them by months and, in one case, a couple of years, though a shock bite, even without a feeding, was sometimes enough to turn the victim.

It was a fact, however, that most vampires could imitate people successfully. So much so that an inexperienced eye would fail to distinguish them right away. Yes, they looked a little unnatural, but even I'd been misled at first. The deaf guy from the seventh floor of Section A had definitely looked more suspicious than Barefoot. While Desi and Didi… I'd followed them through playgrounds and parks across the whole city.

The printer rumbled.

What had Peter called it—"the benefits of vampires in natural conditions"? Well, I'd observed them in natural conditions, even wrote a paper about that. And then Tony even let me publish it. It was about the connection between the better overall state of mental health in regions where the vampire population was retained. No, I didn't tell Peter everything. I didn't mention Didi making a spyhole in the glass in order to throw pebbles at my balcony and call me outside. That first time, I goggled at her and wondered which amulet to hide behind. And she… she was over sixty years old and still reading children's books. I didn't tell Peter that either. Or that I got myself a library card because of her, and that we exchanged books through the nest's mailbox.

I picked up the sheet of paper he had printed and the tape. I unhooked the chain with the crosses and crescents from the balcony door. Turning on the light, I went outside. My fingers froze while I taped the paper to the glass divider. It felt as if someone was drilling a hole into my back, but no matter how often I turned, there was no one on *that* terrace.

I hurried back inside and rehooked the chain. I left the light on, even though vampires had perfect night vision.

LET US
HELP YOU!

The letters were so huge even a human eye could read them from a dozen feet away.

The second half of the hot dog and a box of potato salad later, I realized it was past 7:30; I was finally warm, and the whiskey was having the effect I'd been after all day. Through its golden halo, Maggie and her team looked like friends. They might turn out to be nice enough even in a state of sobriety, at least when they weren't trying to get their way with me, but right now it seemed like a grand idea to tell them all sorts of stories. I quit smoking a couple of years ago and, once the potato salad was splashing around like a greasy ball in my stomach, I ran out of excuses to keep my mouth shut. Worse, all I could think of were stupid shenanigans. If only I had a cigarette!

A rattle on the balcony saved me.

I raised a hand to stop the German gal and Peter. "Lemme!" I peeked through the window, clutching my gold cross.

Rule number one when working with vampires—same one I'd broken at least twice this morning: never take unnecessary risks.

A gray pebble lay on the pristine snow outside. While I inspected it, another one ricocheted off the wall under my window and landed next to the first—*thump*.

I raised my thumb wordlessly.

Only after removing the protective amulets and going outside to the pebbles did I realize that perhaps I should've taken my jacket. I raised my eyes to the broken glass. Behind it, Didi's white face swam like a ghost. The sharp wind tugged at the collar of her nightdress.

"Aren't you… cold?" I asked stupidly.

She shook her head and, contradicting her answer, wrapped her stick-thin arms around herself.

"You understand you're all sick, right?"

Didi bared her teeth at me—huge and ominous, I1 and I2 sticking out: the central upper incisors, her main weapon. She hissed.

At first, I thought she was reacting to my question, but she wasn't looking at me. I glanced over my shoulder: Peter was peering at us from the door.

"No worries, this is a… friend," I said. "He's here with a couple of other friends to help."

"Sss. Sick," Didi spat out. She shivered.

"You're cold. Don't you have a blanket… anything warm?"

"She's not cold, my man," Peter piped up, and threw his jacket over me.

Didi hissed again and swung her head, scraping cheek against shoulder. Her fingers were white with tension, her knuckles jutting: she was clenching her fists as if her life depended on it.

"You're very sick. Very, very sick," I went on. "My friends have brought medicine, but we have to apply it immediately. Otherwise…" I swallowed. "Otherwise the enemies will come and kill you."

Didi tilted her head and slowly rubbed her cheek on her nightgown. In the balcony light, the *vampiris* growth looked like a stain she was trying to wipe off.

"Boom-boom," she mumbled.

"That's right," I nodded. Not that I hadn't played boom-boom with her brothers this morning, but… it wasn't the same, was it?

"We need to give you an injection," said Peter right behind me, startling me. "There's also a cream you need to apply, but the injections are the most important part."

"Cream."

I watched hypnotized as Didi scraped her cheek on her nightgown: back and forth, back and forth...

"It will soothe the itch," Peter said.

"How many of you are awake in the lair?" I asked.

She kept scratching her cheek on her shoulder.

"Didi!"

She hissed and bared her teeth again, but her incisors didn't come out.

"How many of you are awake?"

"Ffffffour." She moved her shoulders.

"The rest are sleeping, yes?" Peter said.

"Sssseven," she nodded and shivered again.

"You have to let us give you injections. All of you."

"Sssssilver!" Didi hissed and moved back a step.

"It's not silver." Peter went around me and looked her in the eye. "Only if you eat us, there will be silver. And boom-boom."

Didi tore her fingers from the sleeve and scratched under her eye.

"If you allow us to give you the medicine, everything will be alright," Peter said. "Now. Immediately."

She watched him, unblinking, and kept scratching.

"We're gonna come in front of the lair," I said. "I'm gonna knock. You put the chain up. Open only enough to poke one arm out. If there's no chain, there won't be any medicine. Then you go to... say, the bathroom. Lock yourselves in. I'll call you out when we're ready. Do you understand me? Didi?"

After a bit, she grabbed her sleeve again and nodded.

"Knock. Chain. Arms. Prick."

"Exactly."

Suddenly Didi spun and sank through the open balcony door into the apartment. She was gone for so long that I began wondering if I should put on the jacket draped over my shoulders. Then I wondered if she'd come back at all. I felt stupid. I left Peter in the middle of the balcony and took down the paper with the plea. Just as I turned holding it, Didi appeared at the hole again.

"Yes. Come. Bring medicine. And cream. We don't eat you—no silver."

"Yes," Peter nodded. "No silver."

"Cross your heart?" Didi stared at me imploringly.

"Cross my heart!" I promised with all the solemnity I could muster.

She might have turned sixty, might even be as old as the Balkan Wars, but she would always remain a child. Not just in height and looks.

"You smell of ours." She pointed at me. "Make yourselves smell of you. Safe. Mmm?" Having read the bewilderment on my face, she shrugged like a human. "Pee on them."

"P—" Peter sputtered.

"Later!" Didi awkwardly spread her fingers and stuck her hand to the glass. There was a patch on her palm, too.

Rule number two in my job: never turn your back on a vampire. In the past, I'd broken that one too, but this time I retreated backwards, squeezing Peter's shoulder to keep him from turning.

I'd kill for a smoke.

For the second time today, I unlocked the door of Section C and waddled into the sea of flyers. The spotlight on my mask sliced the darkness like a Jedi lightsaber. I squeezed my rifle so hard my wound started to pulse again.

"Let Gogo go first?" Peter suggested.

I shook my head, and my yellow saber zigzagged along the opposite wall.

"I've done night missions in Romania," Gogo said. His voice made a faint echo in the mask's headphones.

"Not with mad vampires," Maggie said.

"I'll lead," I said. My stomach might've been throbbing with fear, but I wasn't going to sacrifice another's throat to my own vampires if something went wrong.

By mutual agreement, Sonia, the German, carried the medical bag and traveled in the middle of our formation. Four 50 cc syringes bounced in the pocket of my overalls, and my loins still throbbed from the effort of emptying my bladder to fill them. Pee on them, huh? Easier said…

We silently climbed the stairs to the second floor, then the third. The wind had already blown in a thin layer of snow through the broken window on the landing. I raised an arm to stop the group behind me and leaned the rifle on the railing. Maggie and Gogo covered me, while Peter spun like a masked kid in front of a mirror. I took out the first syringe, removed its needle, and sprayed his bio-suit as uniformly as I could. As I took care of Gogo, laughter started bubbling out of me. By the time I sprayed the dose on Maggie, the five of us, including Sonia, were giggling maniacally.

"In France, we give them the injections during the day," Peter murmured when I picked up my rifle and took the first stair towards the lair. "It's much calmer that way, though some may still be awake."

I swallowed the comment pushing through my

throat. I pointed Gogo towards the apartment with the broken door and Maggie towards the fifth floor. I kept the vampires' place in my sights, ready to bet there was a noise behind the door, but I didn't dare knock until Gogo called out, "Clear!" and Maggie echoed his words.

Without taking my eyes off the door, I nodded and waited until Sonia had prepared the syringes and hoarsely called out, "Ready!"

I unglued my fingers from the weapon and knocked.

The vamp called Pepo giggled behind the door. "Who's knocking?"

I hoped he could smell the rifle bouncing in my hands.

All four headlamps pointed at the door handle. It twitched and the door opened a crack. From the dark hallway came a hissing growl.

"We're not using daylight flashlights," I told the vampires. "But I have one in my pocket, see."

The chain—old-fashioned and yellow—clinked, stretched to the max. A thin hand poked out of the gap. Didi had lost weight but not that much. This hand belonged to a skeleton covered by taut dry skin. I shuddered, seeing a wedding ring taped to a shriv-eled finger.

"Who is she?" I asked, while Sonia left the bag and stepped forward with a syringe in her hand. Gogo moved to her left. We had no illusions about our chances if the vampires decided to spin the shit roulette, but I had no intention of falling without a fight. I felt sick and regretted eating that potato salad.

There was silence behind the door. Finally, Didi spoke up, "Her name is Loretta. You are lying about the flashlight."

"OK, Loretta, now Sonia will touch you. Please stay calm."

I felt like I'd forgotten to breathe as Sonia pressed a thumb against Loretta's forearm, same place where a human would have a vein. I was amazed that she managed to produce a drop of blood. Loretta began growling. I tried to sound cheerful. "All done! You can have your arm back."

Sonia slowly stepped back to her bag.

I heard someone sniffing loudly behind the door, and it closed a little. The chain jangled as if clumsy fingers were trying to remove it.

"I've seen what a daylight flashlight does to vampires," Maggie said. "Compared to that, silver nitrate is downright merciful."

"You're not seriousss," Didi hissed from inside.

"Science is advancing, dear girl," Maggie told her sadly. I was no vampire, but even so, I could see she wasn't lying.

The chain stretched again. The second hand that

showed was male: Pepo, with the silver Seiko on his wrist.

"Won't-ya-give-me something to hold as you poke?"

His teeth chattered, and his hand shook. I barely held in my hysterical laughter as I realized we were not the only ones ready to piss ourselves.

"OK, Pepo, now Sonia's gonna touch you."

He clenched his fist to stop the trembling.

Valyo was third, then Didi reached out through the gap and stoically didn't flinch as Sonia pricked her. She just sniffed the air loudly. "Good. They smell of you!" she said, satisfied.

The door closed, the chain unhooked with a rattle. I gripped my rifle, index finger on the trigger—if the vampires were going to attack us, we were at our most vulnerable now—but all I heard was footsteps shuffling away.

"You can come, we're locking ourselves in," shouted Didi from a distance, and a door was demonstratively slammed.

Click, a key turned.

I shared a look with Gogo, slicing his face with the beam of my headlamp, and kicked in the door. No ambush in the corridor. I turned my head to find the light switch and barely managed to tear my fingers away from the rifle. My whole wrist hurt from the death grip; the wound on the other hand gnawed at me in pulsing bursts… I almost told Peter to take the lead. Almost.

I clicked the switch and flooded the hallway in light.

I wanted to take this as a good sign: someone still paid the electricity bills of my vampires, so there had to be some living Bites around. It wasn't good, though, because just this morning I'd silver-shot an unknown kid in the next apartment, and Loretta hadn't been here at the last winter census.

This was one of the ghosts haunting the *vampiris* plague: crazed with the hunger of the sickness, the diseased ate their herd of human Bites instead of taking care of them, and at the same time, frightened by the weakness and their dying mates, they strove to widen the nest.

"Getting distracted?" Maggie poked me in the kidneys with her air rifle. "Come on!"

I stepped forward, past an empty coat rack with a lonely raincoat. On the left was the kitchen with its empty shelves and dusty cupboards. The thick curtains were drawn tight. Behind them, the windows were nailed shut with plywood, taped over with silver foil. On a bare mattress under the kitchen island slept a girl and a boy, embracing; I didn't recognize them at first. I'd last seen them in the neighborhood this summer—alive.

Peter took the post at the door. Gogo and I pressed our weapons to the vampires' heads while Sonia injected them.

On the right side, the door to the small bedroom was closed. We exchanged positions, Sonia turned the handle and stepped back, but all we found inside were two sleeping vampires, one on the sofa, one cuddled up by the wall. The last three, in the large bedroom, also looked unfamiliar.

Last year, we'd counted twelve vampires in my nest. With the ones I'd killed this morning, I'd seen only six of them so far.

I already knew what we were going to find behind the door of the living room, and I felt thankful for the dry, disinfectant-smelling air I was breathing through the mask.

The shriveled bodies were lined up like logs in the corner.

How many times a night did the living ones go by them?

God!

I stepped back, choking and dry heaving behind the mask.

Something crashed into the inside of the bathroom door.

"Get out!" Didi called out. "You done? Get out!"

Crack! echoed a second hit. A low-pitched growl came from inside, and the vampires scuffled.

Here's a problem from a physics textbook: how much force can a plywood door take before it is broken down by a hungry urban predator?

As we scurried backwards, Sonia dug through her bag, almost crashing into Gogo. She triumphantly got a large plastic box out and left it on the shoe rack.

We closed the front door. I locked it. A crash announced the defeat of the bathroom door.

"The cream absorbs well, it won't stain!" Maggie called out. She was the last of us on the landing.

To my surprise, Didi answered from inside, "OK."

Something thumped into the wall next to the front door. There was no second crash.

Fuck, why had Tony nagged me to stop smoking?

I realized I'd overslept as soon as I saw the light bursting through the thin living room curtains. The granddaddy of all headaches was raging in the expanse of my skull. I felt sick, but the sour taste of puke on my teeth indicated that I'd gotten rid of my dinner at some point during the night. I raised a hand and rubbed my eyes as I noted that I'd slept in my chair, feet on the radiator, and I was all stiff. I blinked at the bandage on my wrist for a good dozen seconds. The wound definitely counted as a *shock bite*. If I didn't want to turn, I had to take care of it and change the bandage. But first I had to get rid of this taste in my mouth and…

The clinking of cups in the kitchen reminded me of something far more urgent: Maggie and her team.

We'd finished my last bottle of whiskey after we'd gotten back from the inoculations. I'd felt as if I would burst with excitement and at the same time, I was light as a feather. We'd laughed and hugged and clinked our glasses—we'd gone into a vampire nest at night and had come back unharmed! Even Sonia had managed to joke in her hybrid English-Bulgarian that she'd shot vampires while awake, but had never had to prick them with a needle.

I lowered my feet to the floor, waited for the pins and needles to pass, and stood up.

"Hey, sleeping beauty!" Peter called from the sofa, making me start. "We didn't expect you to get up this early."

I glanced at my phone—only ten o'clock, so what?—and grinned. "After last night, getting up before noon should be illegal."

Still, I barely had time to reach the toilet bowl and had to hug it for a long time.

When I had rinsed my mouth, brushed my teeth, and taken a shower, I could finally think straight. I carefully unwound the wet bandage and dropped it in the bin. The wound was revolting: puffy, swollen teeth holes, a missing piece of flesh, all of it surrounded by a rich black-and-green-and-yellow bruise. This was a good sign, though. I slathered everything in antibiotic cream from the bathroom cabinet and took out a fresh bandage. This time I didn't tighten it so much; there was no risk it would bleed again. I was considering whether to shave when Sonia called for me to leave my refuge. I took my bathrobe from the door peg, tied the belt as best I could, and decided the razor and I wouldn't see eye to eye today.

I unlocked the door, grinned at Sonia, and made a bet with myself that Maggie and company had managed to find my spare heater and heat up the kitchen. I won. In such cases, I tended to reward myself with pizza, but this time I just mumbled, "Good moaning," and headed for the coffee machine. It was nice not to have your toes freeze as you stared out the window. The plastic bag still waved from the dumpster out there.

"Good morning," Gogo grunted. "Just don't make fun of Sonia, please."

"That's from a TV series," Maggie said, so I didn't have to. She leaned over the sink. "How did you sleep?"

The howl of the coffee grinder—it was out of beans—blocked out my response. I dug out half a pack of whole beans from the cupboard, poured them into the machine, and finally received my dose: hot and aromatic. I pulled out a chair for myself and huddled with the cup. I made a second attempt at a civilized response. "I slept OK, I suppose. Considering how plastered I was last night."

Maggie stifled a giggle and clinked the last plate into the drying rack. After last night's dinner, our tower of washed dishes strongly reminded me of a viral collage on Facebook, suggestively named "Female Tetris."

"Take out the garbage, please," Maggie told Gogo, then picked up a cup and took her turn at the machine.

I expected the kid to start grumbling, but he got up instantly, only requesting that we not eat all the macaroni before he came back. The trash bag from last night was a 30-gallon. I didn't even know I had one of those in the kitchen drawers.

"Macaroni?" I raised my eyebrows.

"With eggs and cheese," said Maggie. "It's a good solid breakfast."

I felt sick at the very thought of food.

"That was so cool last night," she said. "It's the first time I've seen such a connection between an observer and a nest. They like you!"

"Tony will have my head," I muttered. Only when I felt the bare table under my fingers did I realize I'd been looking for a pack of cigarettes.

Maggie brought her cup and sat down next to me.

"He'll use me as a bad example for his students," I said. "How not to observe. Loss of objectivity and all that."

Maggie snorted.

"Either way, he'll have my head." I shrugged and took a sip of coffee. The heavenly first sip! "I'm a collaborationist, a traitor. A loser."

"You're a clown." Maggie grinned at me.

"I'm a pitiful idiot, that's what I am. Take Dave Matthews: he went, gritted his teeth, took photos. While I, at the first trifling matter, collapsed and started wailing in your lap: 'Save my vampires, wah-wah.'"

"Dave shot himself in the head the moment he finished the film montage for Denver," Maggie said.

Beautiful, smart, and with a comeback for every situation?

"That *was* cool last night," I said. "Great thrill and everything, except that, unless your medicine works immediately—"

"It doesn't."

"—we risked our lives for nothing. Once confirmation arrives, Tony will gather the eliminators."

"I know." Maggie stopped smiling and brushed a strand of hair away from her face. Charming, especially with those crow's feet. "Peter is already looking for an appropriate apartment, and last night I informed our headquarters. We'll try to reach an agreement at the top level."

My headache suddenly packed up and evacuated, leaving my head tinkling on empty. "Apartment? You're going to move the nest? In broad daylight?"

Maggie shook her head. "Tonight. We're going to communicate in the same way, and you will lead them to the new place. We have no other choice, you understand?"

I shuddered, despite the heater turning my kitchen into such a cozy place.

"Perhaps a village house," I offered, fully aware I was talking nonsense.

Vampires were city children. They thrived in the natural conglomerations of human beings. What's more, vampires and cities were like the chicken and the egg: I had a theory that, rather than making their nests in the first ancient towns, vampires had stimulated the emergence of those towns. And civilizations. Tony disagreed, but researching this topic was a hobby for my observation-free time. Of which there was a lot.

So, even as I mentioned the house, I knew it wasn't going to happen. I didn't want to imagine a bunch of sick vampires let loose on the outskirts of Mihaylovgrad—let alone awake in a packed building downtown, where the locals would be totally unprepared for their new neighbors. Block 10 was nearly empty for a reason—and no, nobody from the neighborhood had been eaten by vampires.

Well, almost nobody.

Only a few Bites recently and…

Fuck.

My head sagged over the coffee.

Gogo stomped along the corridor with his combat boots and saved the macaroni with cheese and eggs from burning in the oven.

He was promptly followed by Peter, and then Sonia, in charming polka-dot pajamas and fluffy slippers. Who the hell brings nightwear to a suicidal vampire-saving mission?

"Do you want some macaroni?" Maggie asked me. "Can you keep it down?"

Could I? I felt so famished I was ready to start nibbling on the coffee cup. Guess I hadn't kept down any of the potato salad or hot dogs from last night, and two stressful days in a row were taking their toll. The old yearning for a cigarette hadn't reawakened for nothing.

"I think I found an apartment," Peter said five minutes later, after the clack of forks had slowed down enough to allow conversation. "I don't think we should wait for *Sans Changement*[1] to slow down Professor Deliyski."

"Yes, please call and check if we can rent it today." Then Maggie turned to me. "He means Saintangianne, if you were wondering."

The nickname definitely fit Andre Saintangianne, general director of the World Fund. Even the implied reference to the Danube's surroundings fit him: tall, stringy, slightly hunched, devilishly charming, he always showed up at conferences wearing rubber boots and hunting clothes, as if he were on a field expedition, and invariably began his speeches with, "There should be no change for humanity." Just as invariably, Tony foamed at the screen: "There is no change in human stupidity!"

"I doubt even God can force Tony to break protocol," I said. "At most, your boss will piss him off."

"Oh come on. You snapped at me last night, too, when I mentioned the professor… Tony." Peter frowned. "I know he's a little peculiar—"

"—to put it mildly—"

"Fine, he blows his stack out of nowhere and has a habit of screaming his head off at conferences—is that better? Besides, he's a snob—"

"—an egocentric tyrant—" I mumbled. Gogo gig-

---

1 From 1948 until 2016, the Bulgarian National Radio announced the water level of the Danube River every morning, using three languages, one of which was French. Peter refers to the French term *sans changement*, which means "without change."

gled.

"—and he prefers the American methods, but the Sofia Uni folks have done loads of work on the new joint programs, and he hasn't caused any trouble."

"That's true," Gogo said across a mouthful. "Last month he even had a colloquium with our Maggie here."

"About fieldwork," Maggie said. "And about the new system with the online protocols and reports. We've been using the same one in Romania, but only for the last two years, while your results go all the way back to the start and—"

"Wait, wait!" I raised a hand. "You were pulling my leg about this supposed information exchange and blah-di-blah yesterday too."

"And blah-di-blah." Gogo grinned.

"We *are* collaborating," Maggie assured me.

"You and us? The Fund and Tony? Nonsense."

"Honest to God. I can show you letters from the Bulgarian HQ of Without Borders to our official email address and back. I also have records from recent conferences. Less than two weeks ago, we met up with Maya in Constanta about the project with the artificial resettlement." Peter pushed his empty plate towards the middle of the table. "You're at least familiar with the work of the Romanians, aren't you?"

"An absolute, utter madness on the part of those crooks,

quoting my boss, Professor Deliyski," I said.

"Well, I can show you a contract for cross-border cooperation, ratified by him, which says that next spring, the Romanian expertise is going to be applied in Kozloduy, and then in three other cities whose populations have disappeared after the 10th of November."

"Which document do you think I was quoting from?" I waved my fork. "I'm aware alright. Tony even offered me a position in Kozloduy: he said it was the ideal place for me and my theoretical interests. But I'm no theoretician. I'm not interested in punching numbers in a stuffy little office."

"In other words, you don't want to leave your vampires." Peter grinned at me.

"That, too," I said. "Nor am I any good at teaching. I'll leave that to Maya."

A tense silence hung over the kitchen.

"What?" I furrowed my eyebrows.

"You know, right?" Gogo stabbed the last piece of macaroni on his plate. "I mean, that she doesn't have a single intern at the Pazardzhik nest this winter?"

I gritted my teeth. "Those are just rumors."

"I don't know who's taking care of her vampires, but she spent the whole year conquering the academic front. They say she'll become a permanent assistant professor at the Sofia Uni from the spring semester,"

Maggie pitched in.

If Tony had been here, he'd have screamed at them and thrown them out at the first insinuation. I'd give him that: he didn't put up with shit. Me, I just muttered, "Bull."

It had to be bull. Even if it was possible to cover up a case of *vampiris* infection in Bulgaria, Maya wouldn't be able to eliminate her nest on her own. Could one of ours know about it and keep it quiet? No way.

Peter delicately tried to restore the peace. "As I said, you're doing a great job here, and your vampires like you."

"For which Tony will line me up against the wall first."

"For which the hallway stinks of piss to high heaven." Gogo got up and began gathering the empty plates. He put them in the sink and turned to look at us, apparently surprised by the silence. "What? I'll wash all the protective suits; I don't mind. But it was ultra weird for us to make ourselves smell of his piss, right? Never heard of such an approach."

"You probably haven't read the right articles," I said. "They used this method at the very beginning, only with Bites' urine. There were some very interesting studies, but later, safety became the priority, and there were advances in video observation. If a Bite has, um, fed a vampire in the past few days, the vampires won't attack them even inside their lair. And I'm freshly bitten," I waved my bandaged hand. "It's only logical."

"How's the wound?" Maggie pushed that unruly strand of hair away from her face.

"I'm fine. It hurts a little, and there's a huge bruise."

"I'm going to call about the apartment." Peter got up. "You coming?"

"Me? Yeah, why not, I'll just put on something decent." I looked down at my bathrobe.

I'd managed to get into my jeans and dig out a fresh sweater when a quiet chime from the computer announced I had an email. I knew it couldn't be anything good, and I was right.

"They just tightened our noose," I shouted towards the kitchen. "The samples were positive for contagion."

"They're quick, huh." Peter peeked through the door. "Too bad we couldn't buy a bit more time. What's with their tests anyway…"

I pulled on my sweater. Five minutes earlier, I would've thought such news would outright kill me, but now I felt awfully calm. I didn't even crave a cigarette. My phone rang just as I was sticking my head through the neck hole and got to finish the intro of "Tender is the Blood" before I picked up Tony's call.

"Listening, boss." I raised my eyebrows at Peter.

"How are you, son? Did you see…"

"Yeah, I saw it. Well, just as expected. It was complete nonsense to try and prove it with a test anyway."

"I'm very sorry."

I didn't like the greasy sympathy in his voice one bit. Something was off, I could practically smell it.

"Me, too." I sighed.

"I'm gathering the team and we're coming straight to you."

Maggie had joined Peter at the door and was making furious hand signs.

"It's not a fun occasion," I mumbled, "but I'll stop off at the store to get some beer and a couple of grilled chickens."

"What do you mean, beer?" Tony asked. At the door, Maggie kept flailing her arms and pulling faces.

"It's almost twelve," I said, glancing at the clock at the bottom corner of the screen. I mean, I couldn't cut Tony off with *You're the last thing I need today, thanks*. "I'll call the hotel in Vratsa to book rooms for Zhivko and Desi. It's probably not that safe to come down here after dark."

Tony gave a noncommittal grunt.

"But I'll be happy to see you tomorrow!"

Maggie was practically climbing the doorframe by now.

"Don't even plan on getting drunk with Chefo

and Meto," Tony said coldly. "I'll set the meeting for twelve, so we'll have enough margin for any stragglers. Afterwards, well, yes, you'll need moral support, while we deal with the infection."

"Fine, fine. Tomorrow at twelve, got it. Mhmm."

"And you know what?" My boss knew his people and grasped the nuances of my *mhmm*.

"What?"

"No drinking tonight! Not two, not one, and especially not with Chefo."

"Huh?"

For a moment, I wondered if I was overacting, as the silence on the other side grew heavier, but then I heard the grin in Tony's voice, and his fake friendliness made my teeth hurt. "That's my boy. Just so you know, that position in Kozloduy is yours."

"Uh, it's too early for—" I muttered.

"We'll talk about it tomorrow, alright?"

"But really—"

"See you tomorrow." Tony hung up.

I would've laughed if my intestines weren't in a knot. I felt reckless—man, I just conned the boss!—but it also finally clicked that there was no way back. Or forward: there'd be no more hanging out with Chefo, Meto, and the rest. Not tomorrow, not ever.

I stuck the phone in my pocket and said, "Let's go look at the apartment, yeah?"

Peter went out into the hallway. Maggie, however, came into the living room, and as I walked by, she gave me a gentle hug.

Two hours and three viewings later, I hit the brakes in front of the shoe factory. It wasn't three o'clock yet. The actual factory had long been closed, but it had an administrative building that rented out offices. This time around, I was more interested in the canteen, pretentiously labeled a "restaurant." I ordered a schnitzel with vegetables from the girl behind the counter and turned to Peter. "Want anything?"

"I honestly didn't expect us to be sitting down for a bite at a time like this!"

"I'm starving." I took my receipt and moved to the next counter. "Plus, we have another twenty minutes to the next viewing."

"Two pancakes with chocolate," Peter ordered behind me.

The truth was, the shoe factory was ideal for my vampires. At night, the building was empty; during the day, the noise from the nearby sewing workshop and the children's after-school lessons wouldn't bother the vampires. Bites could come and go as part of the normal flow. In total, there were three apartments on the fourth floor of the admin building, all currently available. The factory's director had almost melted like honey in the sun when she heard we wanted to rent. At those prices, it wasn't a surprise.

It took a lot not to snatch the schnitzel with both hands and stuff it into my mouth; instead, I manfully destroyed it with a knife and fork. Next, I dug into the potato side dish and met Peter's stunned look as he began the first cut into his pancake.

"I take my hat off to your metabolism." He blinked at me. "You're skinny like a billiard stick, but I haven't seen you stop eating since yesterday."

"I don't eat like this all the time. Just when I'm stressed," I mumbled. The potatoes were bland, so I shuffled them around and left the dish. I turned towards the woman at the counter. "Will you get me another schnitzel, please? No sides."

Well-fed, I felt better-disposed towards the apartments. I still wouldn't live in them, but the vampires would be safe for the moment.

"I've never had a TV studio in the building," jabbered the factory director as she clacked her heels. "Are you sure the other tenants won't bother you?"

"Are *you* sure the plywood on the windows won't bother you? Ruin the building's façade or something?"

"Oh no, no, no problem at all," she said. "As long as you pay the rent on time. I'll leave the contract with the accountant, so you can sign it when you pay the deposit. Is that OK?"

"We're going to do it in the next hour or two," I said. "And we're going to bring in workers to block up the windows."

"Yes, yes, I understand perfectly. I'll leave the keys with the accountant too."

I turned my gaze to Peter.

The phone vibrated in my pocket, startling me. It was Chefo.

"One moment!" I walked into the next room and cleared my throat. "Hey bro, how's it, bro?"

The speaker buzzed and whistled. It was a familiar symphony, and even before Chefo answered, I knew he was driving and talking. He had the awful habit of ignoring the person he'd called while changing gears or playing with the radio, answering only after you'd screamed his name a couple times.

"Bro?" I tried again.

"How are you holding up?" he asked in a surprisingly sober and serious voice.

"Well, you know…" I feverishly flipped through the available options. "As miserable as they come."

"And do you wanna go shopping?" Chefo said, apparently satisfied I wasn't going to slit my wrists just yet. "Eggs, potatoes, some chicken drumsticks, perhaps steaks."

"I was thinking of doing it tomorrow, all of us?"

"Eh, so tonight we're gonna go hungry?"

"Huh?" I managed, as my stomach dropped into my feet and my heart shot up to my throat.

"What about tonight, I said?"

"What about it? Don't you arrive tomorrow? So the others from the farther regions can join, too."

Chefo snickered. "I'm already past Vratsa, bro. Tony's probably running late, but he and Zhivko took the Petrohan Pass."

"Fuck," I said.

"Come on, aren't you happy to see us?"

I opened my mouth. I closed it. On the second attempt, I blurted out, "D'you have any clue what a mess the house is? If I'd known, I'd have at least cleaned up a little!"

"Oh drop it." Chefo giggled. "We all have piles of dirty socks at home."

The factory director chose that exact moment to peek into the room and announce, "I can't stay any longer, I have some work to do. We're set for later, yes?"

I blinked at her wordlessly.

"Aah, now I see!" Chefo giggled even louder. "Alright, alright, I'm leaving you to 'clean up a little.' Give that particular dirty sock a kiss from me too, alright?" He hung up.

"We're set, yes?" demanded the director.

"Yes, my colleagues will be here soon," I told her and closed my eyes for a moment.

I didn't even wait for the clack of her heels to die down the stairs before calling Maggie. "You need to get out of there, *now*!"

After a sprint through the supermarket and my first cigarette in six years, it was still shortly before 4:00 when I parked in front of Block 10. I wasn't surprised to see Chefo's blue Ford and Meto's red van at the turn-off for the next block. Tony's Mazda appeared behind me, honking, as if it had been waiting for me. It might well have been. I hugged Chefo and Zhivko.

"I took the night train," Zhivko said. "I knew they would confirm."

"Eh." I blinked, mustering my thoughts. The cigarette had left a terrible taste in my mouth. "You could've called, could've asked me to pick you up from Mezdra."

"Going out late at night just to pick me up? Are you bonkers?"

"Have you been smoking?" Tony sniffed at me suspiciously. "No, don't roll your eyes at me. What did we agree, huh?"

Behind his back, Chefo was pulling funny faces, making it hard to come up with excuses rather than laugh out loud. "I lit only one. Probably won't be my last in the next few days. Plus, you told me not to drink."

The truth was that even six years later, there was still no proof that vampires preferred non-smokers or that cigarette smoke bothered them, no matter what my boss claimed. But smoking was undoubtedly out of fashion, and Without Borders was a modern organization, a real skyscraper of steel and mirrored glass.

"Let's go upstairs," Tony groaned.

I unlocked the entrance door and, with a heavy heart, led the group up to my burrow. I'd almost finished climbing the stairs when I finally realized that Meto was rambling on about Maya getting a flat tire and being stuck in Vratsa and running into Nevyana, our colleague from Tarnovo, there.

"It's getting dark," I interrupted him. "Let's call the girls and tell them to get a room."

"What, you got cold feet or something?" Zhivko snorted.

I waved my injured hand, though they couldn't see the bandage under my jacket sleeve. "Yesterday they bit me in broad daylight."

"Is it serious?"

What was I supposed to do? Tell them how much it

hurt despite the salve?

"I'll live." I unlocked the apartment. The lights in the hallway were off. I turned them on.

Apart from the fact that I never turned the lights off, everything else seemed normal.

Zhivko began untying his boots.

"No, no, keep them on," I said. "Coffee?" Without waiting for an answer, I barged into the kitchen.

Suspicious cleanliness reigned everywhere, but at least "Female Tetris" was gone from the drying rack. I turned on the coffee maker so it could heat up.

Someone's hand slapped my shoulder, and I nearly screamed.

"Easy. Now tell your big bro about the chick. Who was she?" Chefo pulled up a chair.

I flipped through a couple of pros and cons in my mind before opening the window and taking out the cigarette pack from my inside pocket.

"You know you can tell me."

I clicked the lighter, took a long drag, and exhaled a cloud. "Her name's Veneta. A manicurist."

"You're shitting me!"

I shook my head and took another drag, expecting my knees to go weak for at least a moment.

"Veneta, huh?"

I balanced my cigarette on the corner of the windowsill and made a double coffee for Chefo.

"Why didn't she do your manicure then?" he probed.

"Because she was *doing* other things, you moron!"

I'd just crumpled the cigarette butt and flung it into the unshoveled snow outside when Zhivko showed up, spinning a rag on his index finger. "Look what I found," he said.

I stared at the pajama top—with polka dots—and felt the bile rise in my throat. First the cigarette, tasting as if a dog had pissed in my mouth, and now this.

"Her name's *Veneta,*" Chefo told him mockingly.

Zhivko critically stretched out Sonia's pajamas and spun it this way and that. It was probably soft and warm, but I'd never seen a less arousing piece of clothing.

"Isn't she afraid the vamps might eat her?" he asked.

I groped for the cigarette pack before answering, "I haven't told her what I do. She thinks I'm a vet."

Chefo had just taken a sip from his cup, so when he started laughing, he sprayed the whole table. Some coffee dripped from his nose too.

My phone chimed elegantly.

"Oooh, Veneta darling?" Zhivko grinned.

It was Maggie, telling me they were on the seventh floor. In the *other* section.

Shipshape! I typed quickly, though there was no

ship, nothing was in good shape, and I absolutely didn't want to imagine what was going to happen when the vampires awakened and smelled them. Nor could I figure out how to escape Tony and Co. after dark. Maybe Veneta would actually come in handy?

I heard my boss raise his voice in the living room. At least he hadn't begun shouting yet.

I looked at the window and into the grayness starting to congeal outside.

Meto appeared at the kitchen door. He'd put on the bottom of his biohazard suit. The sleeves hung down from his waist like a second pair of arms. He raised his eyebrows at us. "What are you waiting for? Tony told us to be ready in five."

"To be ready for what?" I grunted.

Meto raised one of his sleeves pointedly. "For action, what else? Pull on your protection and grab your guns!"

I dashed to the bathroom so fast I beat Chefo to it.

"You and your stomach," Chefo snickered behind me with a nasty undertone.

I would've given him what for if I weren't already typing away on my phone, disguised by the sound of the running water in the sink. The delivery report blinked on the screen.

"Come on! Quit fiddling with that phone," Tony said. "We're all ready, and you haven't even started yet."

"Coming," I said.

"It'll get totally dark, dammit," Chefo muttered.

I splashed my face with water.

Ding! went my phone.

"Stop this childishness right now!" Tony snapped. "The girls are almost here. I'll count to three, and if you haven't come out of the bloody bathroom…"

I flushed and unlocked the door. "What if I haven't come out?" I muttered rebelliously, taking my suit from Chefo and sticking my legs into it. A fireball sagged in my stomach, I felt terribly nauseated, and was really regretting that coffee.

Hold your team off until they awaken, Maggie had written.

One of the few facts established back in the sixties was that vampires strictly followed the solar phases. Under optimal conditions, they awakened at the exact moment of the astronomical sunset and left the world of the living at the astronomical sunrise. As a rule, they hibernated between the fall and spring equinox, regardless of the ambient temperatures. Their appetite and the quantity of their food intake were somewhat influenced by the lunar phases, though the studies carried out since 2006 proved that the variation was mostly due to changes in human blood makeup and activity caused by the lunar cycle. The year before last, there'd been a terrific article by Pedro Cambales in *Vampirical Journal*, called "Do vampires know when blood donation is most beneficial for their Bites?" Since then, I'd been in touch with him. Interestingly, purposeful reproduction also depended on the lunar phases, and not on solar activity: in other words, becoming a vampire was much like ovulation and was almost 20% more likely during a waning or new moon.

Unfortunately, although the abnormal feeding habits of the *vampiris*-infected had been studied in some detail, I'd never come across articles discussing the impact on times of waking and falling asleep for the infected. It was logical, however, that the timing wouldn't change drastically, though the fungus definitely influenced its host's metabolism and activity levels. This did not apply to the infected vampires from yesterday, who hadn't been asleep at all during the day.

Today's sunset should happen around 5:40. I could recite the summer schedule in my sleep, but I didn't follow the winter times so precisely. I didn't dare take out my phone and check; I'd scored enough demerits with Tony as it was.

Three weapon checks later, it was still quarter to five, and I craved a cigarette. A large green Mitsubishi hit the brakes next to the dumpsters outside. Nevyana slid elegantly out of the driver's seat, leaned inside, spun her white-clad butt around, stuck the helmet under her arm, and propped herself up on the front bumper, as if posing for a magazine. Maya wriggled out of the other door more modestly, dressed in a suit unfit for a Hollywood movie and hugging two guns. While Chefo, Meto, and I jointly drooled over Nev—never mind that she was as unreachable as the moon—Zhivko said with forced liveliness, "Apparently, whoever you asked to fix the tires on your car wasn't good for much."

Nev sized him up with a cool look. "He wasn't bad, but the rim was bent. We were going to miss the party."

"Party?" Chefo snorted.

"If we're going to stand around talking, I'll grab my jacket." Nev swept her eyes over the warm outfits of the team.

Tony shook his head. "We're going in. We have half an hour at our disposal, starting," he looked down at his phone, "now. Lead the way!"

I took out my spare key ring and stepped towards the steel door. There was a piece of gum stuck in the lock. I stared at the well-squashed white circle for a couple seconds, absently wondering how I would have explained the disappearance of my keys to Tony if I hadn't had spares.

"What happened, your hand cramped?"

"Kids," I mumbled and moved aside a little, so Tony could see I wasn't messing around.

I tried scraping off the gum with my finger, but the biohazard glove and the negative temperatures meant it was like pulling out a nail with your bare hands. I turned to Meto. "Give me a penknife."

The blade slipped underneath the gum with surprising difficulty, but after I put some force into it, the white disc flew into the air. The slot for the key was also filled with gum, which jutted out like an uneven ridge in the narrow slit. Nobody could scrape *that* out.

"Fuck!" I said frankly.

Tony muttered behind me, "This was not kids, was it?" and struck the front-door window with the muzzle of his gun. I barely had time to pull away. A fragment hit my cheek anyway.

"Heeey!"

Tony leaned down to reach through the thin bars of the welded-on grating and muttered to himself again. He felt along the door and folded himself to peek down.

The inside handle was gone.

"It wasn't a Bite either." Tony squinted thoughtfully. "Meto, check if you can open the grating of the balcony on the right. Is there a ladder somewhere here?" He pointed at the rotten wooden door of the little room by the entrance.

I said, "I have no id—"

"And do you have any idea who stuck their gum there? No, you never have any *idea*! You dig around the forums all day. Why don't you watch porn instead like Zhivko, huh?" Tony kicked the peeling plywood of the door and ripped it out, lock and all. "And who did you send those two messages to earlier? You've done nothing but fool around, you degenerate drunkard!"

I was so dumbfounded I hadn't even reached for the necessary key.

The little room next to the entrance was an old workshop and storage space for some long-gone occupant of the building. Inside there were two ladders: a metal one with three steps and a taller painter's ladder.

"I'm not a drunkard," I said, while Zhivko and Chefo dragged out the tall ladder and Tony showed them where to fit it under the overhang.

"It won't open," Meto called out. "It's welded shut."

"I'm not a drunkard!" I repeated angrily. "And I do my job conscientiously!"

"Is that so?" Tony swiveled around. His face was

twisted into a ferocious grimace. "The whiskey store makes half its sales off you, man!"

"I—"

"Don't you 'I' me! If you had done your job conscientiously, things wouldn't have gotten to this point, because *you'd have finished the nest off yesterday,* instead of arguing with blockheads!" Tony screamed in my face. "What's wrong with you, huh? Instead of acting like a man, you're sitting there whining, and not only do we have to do your job, but you want to leave it for tomorrow!" He imitated me: "'But it'll get dark by the time you arrive!' and 'Why not at midday, why not next Friday…' Come on, move up, before I smack you with the gun."

Zhivko and Chefo stood frozen and wide-eyed behind him.

"What are you staring at, huh? Get your helmets on and go!"

Chefo swallowed. "But Tony—"

"Don't you 'Tony' me! Just look at you, a bigger dunce than the drunkard that almost got killed! And you—why did you rush off to check on your bloodsuckers without even getting your gun, huh, smartypants?"

"But—"

"This loser here at least shot three vampires, but what if yours were awake? What would you have done then, tell me!" Tony held his gun with both hands, the weapon bouncing with his anger. "You can't even pull the trigger on a vampire, can you?"

"But... we can't just..." floundered Chefo.

I'd swallowed my tongue and was grasping my gun so hard I couldn't feel my fingers. How did Tony know what I'd done yesterday? And what about Chefo? What about Zhivko's porn? Or the text messages?

"Are you tapping our phones?" I said at last. "And don't tell me the helmet camera works even when it's not turned on."

"From this whole band of losers, only Maya has some brains!" Tony shouted. The echo was bouncing off the walls of the C-shaped wings of the building and back at my face like I was being slapped. "Did she wait last year for any higher-ups to make the decision, huh? Did she turn it into an international issue, huh? Did she endanger the Balkan population? Huh? And you—how could you invite those twerps, and give them a night tour to boot?"

I was numb with cold and not because of the frigid temperature. I didn't give a shit that he knew about Maggie and the rest. There were other, more crucial questions. I didn't have the strength to turn towards Maya, but I managed to wheeze out, "When was that, Maya? Before or after we counted mine?"

"What does it matter, you piece of trash!" Tony totally lost his shit and poked me in the throat with the muzzle of his gun. "Climb the bloody ladder!"

Of course it mattered. We didn't even know there'd been an infection last winter. At least *I* didn't know.

Of course it mattered: Maya had helped with my census last year. She'd worn gloves around my vampires, but she'd touched the equipment with her bare hands and she might have contaminated it with the fungus.

Meto was already up on the overhang, breaking the staircase window. On full autopilot, I knocked Tony's weapon out of his grip with the muzzle of my own rifle and, to the sound of shattering glass, I hit him in the chest with it once, twice, a third time, screaming through the tears that were freezing on my eyelids, "She infected my vampires, motherfucker! She infected *my* vampires!"

I didn't expect the kick to my groin. I collapsed on the ground. Tony grabbed my hair and drove my face into his knee. The crunch of bone echoed in my skull and cut off the screaming, the tears, even the anger. The pain was so overwhelming I couldn't breathe. Curled up in a ball, I didn't even feel my head hit the tiles, the scrabbling of my gloves on my jacket. Tony kicked me in the ribs—I didn't feel that either; only a tiny part of me coldly observed the bounce of my whole body when his boot connected—then Nev grabbed his shoulder and pulled him towards the ladder. At that moment, a second kick found my back and unfolded me in a mighty spasm. Pain became my whole universe. The last thing the cold observer in me saw was Maya's white trousers stepping over me.

I was not cold. I knew my cheek should have been burning as it rested on the tiles, but my whole face was numb. I was not cold at all, and I didn't understand why my whole body shook. Or at least I didn't understand it until the shivers shifted my head to the point where the pain from my shattered nose burst like fireworks. The blood I was lying in hadn't begun to freeze, but it was sticky.

It took some time to make sure my legs worked, and some more time to struggle to my knees. I stayed like that, panting through my mouth, the icy air burning in my throat. Something important I had to do? I unzipped my jacket and my suit and took out the phone from my pocket. I gave silent thanks that the kicks hadn't hit it as I typed: *They're in.*

Ping, said a phone from my section of the block.

Ping, said my phone in turn. *Come home, I'm waiting inside.*

After a couple of tries, I managed not only to find my feet, but also to get on them. I looked up and, to my astonishment, saw that Chefo had just climbed through the broken window. From the second-floor landing, Tony nagged, "Come on, you laggards!"

I hadn't been down and out on the sidewalk that long.

I trudged to my section. Maggie opened the door and offered me her shoulder. The pain in my groin was dull and pulsating. It wasn't so bad if I walked slightly hunched, but when we started climbing the stairs to the elevator…

"We watched you leave from upstairs," Maya said. "You have keys to the roof, too, which is good. We've prepared a few more small surprises, so we hope to delay your team long enough."

"Did you hear…" I wheezed, while she pulled impatiently at the elevator door.

"I can't believe they've hidden a case of *vampiris*, I really can't!" Maggie shook her head and stabbed the button for the eighth floor.

"I can." I leaned on the back wall of the elevator. "For Tony, success in the scientific field is the be-all and end-all. And what success can we have if we allow an infection to spread, and half of Without Borders start breathing down our necks?"

We'd passed the fifth floor before Maggie spoke up.

"I know what he's like, but this is…"

I dragged myself out of the elevator and up the ladder to the attic, and then to the roof. The wind almost pushed me over. In some areas, the snow had blown off, and in others we crunched through snowdrifts. I waded through an actual puddle, apparently melted by the sun during the day. Maggie kept helping me, while I clenched my teeth. Nevertheless, I slipped on the thick layer of ice around a chimney, my glove scrambling comically over the chimney wall before I fell to my knees and cracked my head on its edge.

That wasn't comical. And it hurt like hell.

We crawled over the frozen section on our hands and knees, while the wind pushed us further and further to the side.

Only when I grabbed onto the next chimney and managed to stand up did I realize we'd ended up less than two feet away from the edge. The wide tongue of ice flowed over it, and there, at the precipice, there was nothing to clutch at.

I automatically patted my pocket—somewhere, under the protective suit, was my cigarette pack—but I didn't even feel like smoking. As if Tony had finally beaten the desire to light up out of me as well as shattering my nose.

Heroically, I tried not to let my teeth chatter while we squeezed ourselves through the attic trapdoor of

Section C. Now I was finally cold—totally, unbearably cold, except for my sinuses, which felt like they were being stabbed by a hot poker with each shiver.

We slid down the metal stairs. Peter was waiting for us and held me upright.

Pop! an air gun coughed somewhere below. *Pop!*

Peter and Maggie pushed me into the left-side apartment. They closed the door.

"He knows we're here," she panted. "He's apparently tapping your phones. And your mail."

"And the camera transmits even when it's off." I would've knocked on my helmet but I'd dropped it somewhere. Perhaps on the sidewalk. I honestly couldn't remember.

"Sonia will hold them downstairs for a few minutes. We barricaded her behind some ripped-off doors." Peter grinned. He held up a packet of 50 cc syringes and passed me a large glass. "Chop-chop."

I stared at the glass, then realized what he was asking for.

"Do you think it'll work?" I mumbled, but I opened the bathroom door—luckily it was right next to the front door—and tried to convince myself that attempting to piss wasn't going to hurt.

Yeah, right. I was surprised it wasn't blood that flowed into the glass. The stream wasn't even pink. Hopefully, the kicking I'd received would leave only bruises.

The blood on my cheek had dried and was pulling at my skin. I passed the full glass to Peter and only then did I realize that my rifle was gone.

While Peter and Maggie transferred my urine into the syringes, Gogo was waiting for me with two pills and another glass, this one full of water. A thick turtleneck showed through the open zipper of his suit, along with a holster holding a weapon. A real one. My eyes were glued to the rounded butt while I dropped the pills on my tongue and drank. My nose was so swollen I almost choked—I couldn't take a breath between gulps.

Peter sprayed Maggie with the first dose, and Gogo spun in front of him like a model for the second.

"Come on, hurry up!" Maggie told me and, without waiting for the pills to kick in, we ran out and rushed down the stairs.

Well, they rushed. I trudged at the very back.

Pop! Ptarrp! coughed the air gun for the last time, and Sonia screamed, "Run!"

I didn't know if it was a cry for help or a warning, but a crash from the stairwell hinted that the door-barricade had been overcome.

"You, here," I heard Tony command.

"But," Chefo stammered, "we don't have time! We need to lea—"

"Then leave!" Maya snapped. "What are you waiting for? Dump your mates and save your skin!"

I didn't hear the click of the key, but the chain tinkled: they'd opened the apartment.

"I'll fucking kill you all!" yelled Tony.

The door to the lair crashed into the wall. Was Tony the one who had kicked it in?

Meto squealed like a woman at a mouse. *Pop! Pop! Pop!* coughed several guns at once, and the whole stairwell glowed with a white radiance.

The sun had set.

"Fuck!" Peter hissed one floor below me.

Five steps farther, I'd completely forgotten about my aches and pains. Nev yelled, "No!"

An air gun popped but no radiance followed.

Gogo had taken a position between the landing and the fourth floor. I passed him in time to see a barely outlined Chefo dash out of the nest-apartment—the beam of his headlamp burning holes in the walls—trip over something soft and motionless (*Sonia,* the cold observer inside me registered; it *had to* be Sonia) and fall down the stairs headfirst. He didn't make a sound. Someone inside the nest was screaming, "Fuckfuckfuckfuckfuck!" and two shots merged into one. This time, there was a radiance: a vampire was burning. I got down the last stairs, and the flickering light revealed a picture from hell: three vampires had grabbed Meto and were dragging him in different directions, blood spurting from his neck, his daylight flashlight shining straight up at the ceiling. Zhivko was at Meto's feet, on his knees; he didn't look hurt. Peter was trying to shove away his attackers with his rifle. Tony had almost reached the bathroom and was about to enter when Didi grabbed his weapon and ripped it out of his hands. Behind him there was someone else—Maya?—and at the threshold of the bedroom I saw Nev's perfect white legs. Above her, a vampire had just about burned out.

As I opened my mouth to shout, I realized how stupid it was. And yet…

"Stop!"

Meto slumped, right on top of Zhivko, who began shrieking like a little girl. Two vampires turned towards me as one, bared their teeth and hissed, but didn't attack. Outlined by Maya's headlamp, Tony had his weapon back and was desperately trying to reload, while Didi watched him, motionless.

"Drop it," Gogo commanded coldly from behind me.

In the bathroom, Maya's beam turned. Behind her, I saw a silhouette curled up in the corner. It didn't move, didn't try to lunge at her…

"Don't!" I shouted at Maya.

Too late.

Pop! said her weapon. The burst of light blinded us. Didi dove under Tony's arm—faster than the human eye could follow—knocked Maya over, and the bathroom filled with a wet sound, which was going to haunt my nightmares for a long time. Tony dropped the pneumatic magazine with silver nitrate—his hands were shaking so badly. He dug through his pockets for a jet injector.

Bang! Gogo's handgun boomed behind me.

The shot was deafening; the echo, twice as loud.

"Argh!" Tony gurgled just like in the comics. Blood gushed from his shoulder; the syringe fell at his feet. His eyes were wide as saucers. A huge vampire literally flew out of the main bedroom and almost got him, but Maggie threw herself at the monster's back and knocked him down. His inarticulate roar was also going to haunt me. The two rolled on the floor, clinging to each other.

Zhivko shot forward like a snake, and the vampire curled away from Maggie. A headlamp beam highlighted the syringe driven into a bare, stiffening leg. A second convulsion and the monster jerked up, mouth foaming with blood, claws digging into the walls. Then, nothing. He didn't burn, he simply froze in an overpowering seizure.

"To the kitchen. Now!" Gogo hissed behind me.

"To the kitchen!" I repeated mechanically, while

Peter slid past Meto's recent attackers, hugging the wall.

The vampires… obeyed me. To some extent. One went back inside. The other—Pepo with the Seiko—also took a step in that direction but watched Peter with the unblinking gaze of a reptile.

Maggie carefully helped Tony to his feet. He'd gone paper-white and staggered.

She took a step, then a second.

Everything will be fine, I told myself and swallowed my heart, which had fluttered up to my throat.

Then Tony dug his uninjured hand into his pocket and brought out some kind of ball.

One second stretched like treacle: I stared blankly at the object between his fingers, wondering what he was doing. Maggie screamed "No!" and pushed Tony forward. He threw the ball to the floor and fell on his face with a muffled scream.

Peter lunged at Pepo and pushed him back towards the kitchen. The vampire didn't even hiss, just opened his maw wide.

Light flashed.

No. The light *bathed* the whole apartment in white. For a split second, like a negative, my retina was imprinted with Pepo's skeleton digging its fingers into Peter's shoulders and his teeth into Peter's throat. The vampires didn't burn—they literally evaporated. An unbearable smell rolled over me: crunchy, charred meat layered over the choking taste of decay and rotting flesh. That was exactly how I imagined the A-bomb over Hiroshima.

By the time the ball had burned out, I was on my knees, covering my face with my hands, retching in vain. I'd probably further dislocated my nose; the pain was excruciating.

"A sunlight grenade," I heard Gogo mutter behind my back.

I blinked in a futile attempt to adjust my eyes to the darkness once again sliced only by Gogo's headlamp. A hand prodded my shoulder, but I failed to scream. Only a muffled groan made its way out of my throat.

"Hold it, dammit!" Gogo poked me harder.

Stupidly, I reached backwards and spent another couple of seconds staring even more stupidly at the flashlight I was holding onto like a lifebelt. I finally clicked it. Gogo stepped around me and squatted next to Peter, who was slumped by the wall, covered in fine black ash. The Seiko balanced ridiculously on his shoulder, its strap empty. Blood gushed from Peter's throat like a fountain, but he was still alive and trying to breathe. Gogo muttered some comforting nonsense while slapping a thick bandage on the wound. The Seiko slid down and splashed into the puddle of blood turned crimson in the light of the headlamp.

I shone the light at Tony, who was doubled over and trying to stand up. His left hand hung lifelessly. Blood dripped from his fingers. His face under the crooked helmet was twisted into a terrible grimace. His headlamp had shattered when he fell.

Behind him, Zhivko's boots stuck out. He wasn't moving. Why wasn't he moving?

I couldn't see Maggie anywhere. I started panicking and hyperventilating, the hideous taste of burned meat coating my throat. I struggled to my feet. Zhivko's back was sprinkled with ash but I couldn't see any blood; I hadn't seen anyone attack him either, I had not… He twitched and rolled heavily to his side.

"No, no, don't." Maggie was in the bathroom, cajoling in an astonishingly calm, soft voice. "Look, honey, I'm not prey, I smell good."

"Didi!" I wheezed out and finally managed to get to my feet.

So did Tony.

I was engulfed by the excessively stupid feeling that I was a gunman in the Wild West. Wrapped in a coat of cold calmness, I stared into Tony's eyes, and despite the dim light, I could make out each eyelash, each wrinkle around his eyelids, each muscle twitch.

"You bloody Bite!" Tony spat out. The disgust in his voice lashed me like a whip. A day earlier, it would have hurt me. I would have trembled. Felt faint. Now

I only licked off the blood running down my lip and kept staring into his eyes.

"Get out of my way, you stupid son-of-a-bitch!" Tony stepped forward.

A day earlier, I would have let him pass. Asked questions. Made excuses. Now I simply did not take my eyes off him, and as soon as he squinted slightly, I didn't even wait to see the hand he'd hidden behind his back.

My kick got him right in the groin. My combat boots had steel toes. Tony's legs folded cartoonishly, and he took an eternity to fall forwards. I expected him to hold a knife or a scalpel, but his hand came out empty. I kicked once more anyway, and my boot met his cheek. He flew sideways, hit the wall, and fell on top of Meto's body.

A day earlier, I would have felt guilty. Now I just passed him by and leaned over Zhivko. I grabbed his shoulders and helped him sit up. His eyes were empty. Next to the entrance door, Gogo sobbed.

I patted Zhivko's cheek. "Get the kid outta here. Check the woman on the stairs and find Chefo, alright?"

For a second he stared at me unseeingly. Then he nodded and began to move.

In the bathroom, Maggie was still cooing reassuringly. I entered slowly.

Curled in the corner, Didi was half-hidden by Maya's corpse. The wall and floor were all covered in ash: the remnants of another vampire—the one who had protected Didi from the light of the grenade. Didi raised her head, looked at me: a little girl with a stained blue nightie and disheveled black hair. She might have been as old as the Balkan Wars, but she would always remain a child.

Didi reached out. So I could help her get up.

THE END

ACKNOWLEDGMENTS

When I go on expeditions in others' minds, I bring back souvenirs. This story is one of them. So I owe my most heartfelt thanks to Elisabeth Colbert for igniting the spark, and to Kalin M. Nenov for helping push it past the point when I was going to give up and go the easy way. Thanks are also owed to Lyuben Kozarev, to Vesela Proshkova, and, of course, to Roberta Bassarbolieva, who helped a lot in recreating this story in English, and to Simon McLeish for proofreading this and many other translations. And that is just the Bulgarian team. Thank you for believing in my urban predators, Mr. R. B. Wood, my editor Maria Haskins, and all the wonderful people at Ruadán Books who brought my vampiric child to life. My gratitude also to Alex Shvartsman, whose guidance is priceless.

And thanks to my Mom for everything. This story was written before she came to live with me, so she didn't share the joy and frustration of its creation. My house is emptier by one Mom now, when the urban predators are being published, but she's here, in my heart. Always.

ABOUT ELENA PAVLOVA

Elena Pavlova lives in Montana, Bulgaria, and is the author of numerous short stories, novels, fiction collections, and game books. Her short stories have appeared in various Bulgarian publications, winning awards from national competitions, while two of her novels have received prestigious awards: Bulgaria's National Konstantin Konstantinov Award (2019) went to „Камен и пиратите от 5г" (*Kamen and the Pirates from 5-B*) and the ESFS's Best Work for Children Award (2021) went to „Коледари срещу хали" (*Christmas Carolers vs Hallus Beasts*). She is also an accomplished translator and has translated into Bulgarian authors as diverse as Robert Howard, Robert R. McCammon, and Peter Watts. Her short stories have appeared in *Samovar, Asimov's Science Fiction,* and *Night Shades,* among others. In 2021, she was awarded the SLF's Diverse Worlds Grant.